HERO

ATLANTIS QUEST

ATLANTIS ASSAULT

Steve Barlow and Steve Skidmore

Illustrated by Jack Lawrence

First published in 2014
by Franklin Watts

Text © Steve Barlow and Steve Skidmore 2014
Illustrations by Jack Lawrence © Franklin Watts 2014
Cover design by Jonathan Hair

Franklin Watts
338 Euston Road
London NW1 3BH

Franklin Watts Australia
Level 17/207 Kent Street
Sydney, NSW 2000

A CIP catalogue record for this book
is available from the British Library.

pb ISBN: 978 1 4451 2873 3
ebook ISBN: 978 1 4451 2874 0
Library ebook ISBN: 978 1 4451 2875 7

1 3 5 7 9 10 8 6 4 2

Printed and bound by CPI Group (UK) Ltd, Croydon, CR0 4YY

Franklin Watts is a division of Hachette Children's Books,
an Hachette UK company.
www.hachette.co.uk

How to be a hero

This book is not like others you may have read. You are the hero of this adventure. It is up to you to make decisions that will affect how the adventure unfolds.

Each section of this book is numbered. At the end of most sections, you will have to make a choice. The choice you make will take you to a different section of the book.

Some of your choices will help you to complete the quest successfully. But choose carefully, some of your decisions could be fatal!

If you fail, then start the adventure again and learn from your mistake.

If you choose correctly you will succeed in your quest.

Don't be a zero, be a hero!

The quest so far...

You are a member of a Special Forces naval unit. You are an expert diver and can pilot submarines of all types. You are a specialist in underwater combat and have taken part in many dangerous missions. Your bravery and skill have won you many medals.

You have been recruited by Admiral Crabbe, leader of ORCA — The Ocean Research Central Agency. Your mission is to defeat the Atlanteans, a race of amphibians who are determined to destroy humankind.

To help you in your quest you have been given command of the Barracuda, the most advanced submarine in the world. The Mer, another amphibian race, created this amazing machine. The Mer are sworn enemies of the Atlanteans and have an alliance with humankind.

TOP SECRET: ORCA Barracuda

(1) Stunfish launcher –
self-propelled weapons resembling
sunfish that produce a low-frequency
sonic wave to knock out enemy
defences.

(2) Crew cockpit –
where the Barracuda
pilots sit.

(3) Countermeasures –
ultra-fast mini-rockets that
target and destroy enemy
torpedoes.

(4) Water cannon –
fires a super-heated water
jet at close range, which
is hot enough to cut
through metal.

(5) Torpedo tubes –
launch supercavitation
torpedoes with
explosive warheads.

**(6) Sub-aqua
bike bays –**
pods for launching
the sub-aqua bikes.

(7) Propulsion system –
powers the sub through the water.
Also capable of a short 'jet boost'.

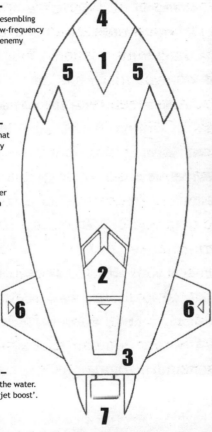

THE ATLANTEANS:

A race of amphibians, who once lived in the legendary city of Atlantis. Masters of sea-based technology.

HOME:

New Atlantis, a realm under the sea floor.

TRITON: King of the Atlanteans

OBJECTIVE: To destroy humankind and take over the Earth.

HISTORY:

Hundreds of years ago, the Atlanteans declared war on humans. With the Mer's help they were defeated. Entrance to Atlantis is guarded by the Mer.

BACKGROUND INFORMATION:

The Atlanteans have broken out from New Atlantis. They have declared war on humans and the Mer.

With the help of Shen, a female Mer, you have already defeated three Atlantean commanders, Hydros, Hadal and Tempest. You have also captured a pressure shield generator, which allows the Barracuda to operate at unlimited depths, and a defensive shield, which increases your vessel's ability to survive attack.

In your latest battle you managed to salvage a cloaking device. With the help of Shen's father, Admiral Merrow, you have fitted this device to the Barracuda. It has made the super sub practically invisible.

However, during the battle of Mer City, Shen was captured and taken to New Atlantis. You have promised to rescue her, and to help the Mer have given you their most powerful weapon — a deadly seaquake device.

You must reach New Atlantis through the hole in the seabed where the Atlanteans have broken out. Once in the city, you must rescue Shen and escape before sealing the hole. Only then will humankind be safe from the Atlanteans.

The future of the Earth is in your hands... Go to 1.

1

You have been searching for a way into New Atlantis for some time. You know that unless you manage to locate the hole in the seabed, Shen will be lost forever.

Suddenly the Barracuda's computer voice breaks the silence. "Atlantean vessel two kilometres ahead."

A 3-D image fills the screen. It is a Starfish cruiser, a powerful sub, armed with many explosive spines. You know that the Barracuda's new cloaking device means that the enemy will not be able to see you.

If you wish to attack the cruiser, go to 16.
If you wish to follow it, go to 37.

2

You decide that you will have to tell Triton the location of the Barracuda in order to save Shen's life.

"Very well." You hand over the homing device. "This will take you to the Barracuda. The seaquake device is on board."

"I knew you were bluffing," smiles Triton.

"Humans are weak."

"I've told you where the device is, now let us go."

Triton laughs. "Humans are also too trusting." He hurls his trident at you. It pierces your chest and you sink to the floor. "I now have the seaquake device and Merrow's daughter," he cries. "Earth will soon be ours!"

They are the last words you hear.

Why did you trust Triton? Go back to 1.

3

You decide to try to sneak into New Atlantis through the doors. You carefully edge the Barracuda forwards. With the cloaking device active you know the super sub is invisible. An Atlantean supply sub steers towards the gateway and the doors begin to open. You follow closely behind, but just as you are passing through, the doors slam shut. The Barracuda's hull is crushed between the doors, and water floods the cockpit.

Your quest has failed. Go back to 1.

As the water drains from the lock and the destroyer begins to sink downwards, you carefully move to the side of the vessel, making sure that you are not spotted.

Soon the airlock is ready — with water filling the lower part — and the gates open. The destroyer floats into the dome towards a vast harbour. There are hundreds of Atlantean warships in the dock.

You see a small quay that is deserted and make your way towards it. You test the air in the dome and find it is breathable, so you emerge from the water and retract your aquasuit helmet.

You now have to find Shen. Your navigation systems don't work in New Atlantis, and you wonder how you will find her in this vast city. As you consider what to do next an Atlantean guard suddenly appears. He sees you and reaches for his dart gun.

If you wish to kill the Atlantean, go to 24.

If you wish to try to capture the guard, go to 12.

5

You steer the Barracuda through the shoal and the creatures move out of your way. Suddenly you realise you are making a big mistake. By passing through the shoal, the outline of the Barracuda is clear for any enemy to see!

You look out — the Atlantean patrol is heading towards you.

If you want to speed up and hope the enemy doesn't spot you, go to 47.

If you want to attack the patrol, go to 33.

6

The Ray fighter is almost upon you as you fire a sea dart missile. It crashes into your enemy and detonates. The fighter explodes and the shock wave sends you spinning from the bike.

As you float away dazed, a patrol of Atlantean guards, mounted on cyborg seahorses, heads towards you. It is the last thing you see before you black out.

Go to 23.

7

You wait for the shark to close in and then dodge out of its way. Thankfully, the shark swims over and begins to feed on its dead Atlantean rider. You decide that you don't want to end up like the Atlantean, so you leave the shark well alone. That was a close call!

Go to 40.

8

You realise that the Atlanteans will try to hunt you down, rather than head for the rift in the seabed. You will have to make them think that the Barracuda has been destroyed.

You order the Barracuda to fire a couple of Stunfish torpedoes. You know that the Atlanteans will use them to lock onto your present position.

Seconds later the Barracuda gives a warning. "Incoming SMART torpedoes."

"Launch countermeasures. Taking evasive action," you say, calmly.

The Barracuda's mini-rockets dart towards the enemy torpedoes as you spin the super sub away. The incoming torpedoes are destroyed in a huge explosion that lights up the water.

You wait for some time. Finally, the Atlantean ship moves away. Your plan has worked! The Atlanteans think the explosion of the countermeasure rockets was your sub being destroyed! You can now follow the enemy vessel to the hole in the seabed.

Go to 37.

9

"Let's attack that Tiger shark," you say as you swing the Barracuda around. You launch a stream of torpedoes at Triton's shark. At the same time the Atlantean fleet launch hundreds of torpedoes at the Barracuda.

"Incoming!" cries Shen.

Your torpedoes hit Triton's cyborg shark and explode, sending the Atlantean leader to oblivion. However, you don't have long to savour your victory. Seconds later, the Atlantean torpedoes hit the Barracuda, blowing it apart.

You destroyed Triton, but failed to seal the hole in the seabed. Ultimately, you have failed! Go back to 1.

10

You decide to take the seaquake device with you. You don't know how long it will take you to rescue Shen, and you don't want to get caught in the explosion if you don't make it back in time.

You clip the seaquake device to your aquasuit.

If you chose to take the sub-aqua bike, go to 18.

If you chose to take the DPV, go to 31.

11

You decide to capture and use the cyborg shark
to help you get into New Atlantis.

You speed towards your enemy, gun ready.
The guard doesn't see you coming and you
quickly deal with him. As the Atlantean floats
from the shark, the cyborg creature spins
around, mouth open, revealing rows of razor-
sharp teeth. It speeds towards you.

**If you want to shoot the shark with your
jet gun, go to 32.**

To try to dodge the shark, go to 7.

Before the Atlantean can move you fire a stun grenade from your jet gun. It explodes in front of the creature and knocks him backwards. You move forward and quickly remove his weapons. Then you bind his hands. The Atlantean groans.

"I know you can hear and understand me. You are going to tell your superiors that I am here and I have the power to destroy your city. I wish to be taken to Triton. If I am not, then New Atlantis and all its people will be wiped out."

He nods slowly, and then begins to talk into his comms device.

Minutes later a group of Atlantean soldiers appear in a Flying fish hovercraft. They leap out of the vehicle and point their guns at you. You drop your jet gun and smile.

"Glad you could come to the party," you say. "Take me to your leader."

Go to 38.

"Scan the entrance," you order the computer.

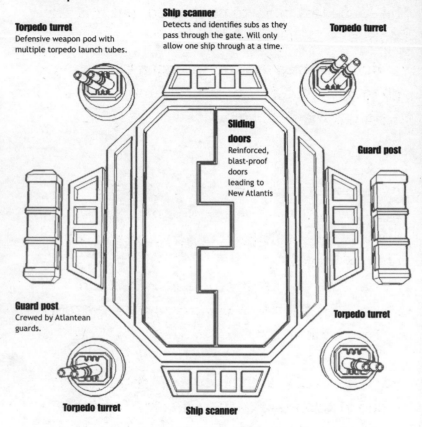

Ship scanner
Detects and identifies subs as they pass through the gate. Will only allow one ship through at a time.

Torpedo turret
Defensive weapon pod with multiple torpedo launch tubes.

Torpedo turret

Sliding doors
Reinforced, blast-proof doors leading to New Atlantis

Guard post

Guard post
Crewed by Atlantean guards.

Torpedo turret

Torpedo turret

Ship scanner

You curse. You realise that even with the cloaking device you will not be able to sneak into New Atlantis in the Barracuda — but Shen is in there! If you are going to get into the city you will have to use a sub-aqua bike or the Mer DPV (Diver Propulsion Vehicle) Admiral Merrow gave you. The DPV is smaller than the sub-aqua bike, and less likely to be spotted, but it is also slower.

If you wish to use the sub-aqua bike, go to 39.

To use the DPV, go to 35.

14

As the water floods from the airlock, the destroyer begins to sink downwards. You realise that the hull will crush you if you don't get out quickly.

You open up the throttle on the DPV and shoot along the floor, just avoiding the bottom of the Lionfish.

You emerge at the front of the vessel, but your desperate escape has been spotted! A group of Atlantean warriors emerge from the destroyer and head towards you.

If you wish to fight the Atlanteans, go to 36.

If you decide to surrender, go to 43.

15

You cut power to the DPV and float in the water. The Ray fighters spin away — they hadn't seen you! You breathe a sigh of relief, and restart the DPV.

In the dark you glide towards the Lionfish destroyer waiting in the queue. As you think about how you will get into the city, you see a lone Atlantean guard mounted on a cyborg shark.

If you wish to continue towards the
Lionfish destroyer, go to 40.

If you wish to try to capture the shark,
go to 11.

16

You decide to attack the Atlantean sub. "Lock
on torpedoes," you order. "Fire!"

Two torpedoes speed towards the Starfish
cruiser and hit the enemy ship. However, they
just bounce off the hull. The cruiser has a
strong defensive shield! You are going to have
to disable it to destroy the enemy ship.

If you wish to move in closer and continue
the attack, go to 25.

If you wish to abandon the attack on the
cruiser, go to 45.

17

"We'll use the seaquake device," you tell Shen.
"There are two minutes left until it blows."

"But that will destroy New Atlantis," she
replies. "You gave your word to Triton."

"And I'm breaking it," you reply. Despite

Shen's protests, you load the device into a torpedo tube and launch it.

Before you can hit jet boost, a huge explosion vaporises Triton's Tiger shark and breaks open New Atlantis's dome. The seabed is blasted apart and the sea quakes.

The Barracuda is hammered as thousands of tonnes of rock crash onto it, burying the super sub, and both you and Shen forever.

You broke your word and have paid dearly for it. Go back to 1.

18

You slip out of the Barracuda on the sub-aqua bike and head towards the dome of New Atlantis.

There are many Atlantean ships waiting to get into the dome, and patrols of Atlantean guards mounted on cyborg seahorses and sharks.

Suddenly, the bike's computer beeps out a warning. You glance to your left and see a Ray fighter moving towards you at speed. You've been spotted!

If you wish to attack the Ray fighter,
go to 6.

If you wish to try to hide, go to 44.

19

You head towards the side of the Lionfish
destroyer and come to rest beside one of the
gun mountings.

The gates to the dome open up and the
vessel begins to move forwards. You hold onto
the hull as the ship passes through the gateway.

Suddenly, an alarm goes off — you've been
spotted! You spin around, but you are too
late. The gates slam shut. You are trapped! A
squad of Atlantean fighters emerge from the
destroyer and head towards you.

If you wish to fight the Atlanteans, go
to 36.

If you decide to surrender, go to 43.

20

You open up a comms channel to ORCA HQ.
Within seconds, Admiral Crabbe's face appears
on the screen. You tell him about the canyon's

location.

"Good work," he replies. "We'll get our forces there as soon as possible. I'll inform the Mer, so they can send troops. You've done what you needed to do. Wait for reinforcements to arrive. We'll need the Barracuda to lead the attack."

The line cuts out. You think about what you should do. Shen is still a captive and you promised to rescue her. However, Admiral Crabbe has given you an order.

If you wish to go into the rift to find Shen, go to 29.

If you wish to obey Crabbe's order and wait, go to 42.

21

"If you kill her I will never reveal the location of my sub," you tell Triton. "Your kingdom will be destroyed. Are you prepared to risk that for the life of a human and a Mer?"

Triton considers. "Very well. You can leave. Release the prisoner," he tells his guards. He points at you. "We will meet again, human. Do

not think this is over between us."

Soon you and Shen are heading to the airlock. You retrieve the DPV. "You realise that Triton will follow us," says Shen.

"That's not what is worrying me," you say. "We have less than thirty minutes to get to the Barracuda and switch off the device."

The Atlanteans allow you to leave the dome, but you know they are following your movements.

You use the tracking device to locate the Barracuda and board the super sub. You stand over the seaquake device and check the countdown clock. "Ten minutes left. That was close!"

At that moment the Barracuda sounds an alert. "Incoming vessel. Royal cyborg Tiger shark."

"It's Triton," says Shen. "What do we do?"

If you wish to use the seaquake device and blow up New Atlantis, go to 17.

If you wish to head up to the hole in the seabed, go to 34.

You follow the Atlantean ships towards the city.

Ahead of you is a line of subs, queuing up in front of two giant doors, leading into the dome. The doors open up, allowing only one ship in before slamming shut.

If you wish to sneak your way in, go to 3.

To scan the entrance to New Atlantis, go to 13.

23

You wake to find yourself lying on the floor of a vast room. Triton stands in front of you with a familiar figure beside him.

"Shen!" you cry out. You try to get up, but you are too weak.

Triton laughs. "So, at last you wake."

"Shouldn't you have killed me?" you ask.

"I wanted to see the human who was responsible for the deaths of my commanders, and to inform you that you have failed. Your sub has been found and we have your device."

"What about Shen?" you ask.

"I will use her as ransom against the Mer. Without their support you humans are helpless against us. And now I will grant your wish!"

Before you can reply, he hurls his trident at you. It pierces your chest and you pass into blackness.

Triton has made his point! Go back to 1.

24

You draw your weapon, but are too slow. Your enemy shoots a razor-sharp dart into your chest. With a cry you drop to the floor. You try to return fire, but another dart pierces your body, sending you into darkness.

You got into New Atlantis, but ultimately failed! Go back to 1.

25

As you steer the Barracuda towards the enemy, its alarm begins to sound.

The water around you is lit up as dozens of explosions rock the super sub. Though they cannot see you, the Atlanteans have launched hundreds of torpedoes and depth charges towards you. They hope that at least some will hit you.

Before you can take evasive action, the Barracuda is struck by a deadly shockwave. Even your defensive shield cannot withstand such overwhelming firepower.

"Defensive shield compromised," warns the Barracuda, but it is too late. Another salvo of torpedoes strikes, sending the Barracuda to the bottom of the ocean.

To see if you can defeat Triton, head back to 1.

You glide down and settle yourself under the hull of the Lionfish destroyer. The gates to the dome open up and the vessel's engines burst into life.

It moves forward into the airlock. Ahead of you are two huge glass-like doors. Through them you can see the city of New Atlantis.

The metal gates shut behind the Lionfish. Without warning, water begins to empty from the airlock.

If you wish to stay hidden under the destroyer's hull, go to 14.

If you wish to move out from your hiding place, go to 4.

27

You choose to leave the seaquake device in the Barracuda and set it to detonate, just in case you don't make it back. That way at least New Atlantis will be destroyed, even if you fail in your mission to get Shen back.

You set the seaquake device to explode in five hours and arm it. The countdown begins.

If you chose to take the sub-aqua bike, go to 18.

If you chose the DPV, go to 31.

28

"Before we jet boost, load the seaquake device into a torpedo tube," you tell Shen. "Set it to detonate on impact!" She quickly does so.

You hit jet boost and shoot towards the exit. The Atlantean fleet opens fire and the water is filled with a mass of torpedoes, mines and depth charges. The Barracuda is flung about in a whirlpool of explosions.

"Triton has launched a SMART torpedo," warns Shen.

The exit is just ahead.

"Firing the seaquake device!" you say.

As you shoot through the hole in the seabed, the seaquake device strikes the edge of the canyon above you and detonates. The Barracuda catches the edge of the massive explosion and is tossed aside like a leaf in a storm. Triton's incoming SMART torpedo is vaporised, and so is his Tiger shark and Triton himself!

Millions of tonnes of rock tumble from the shattered wall of the canyon, blocking up the hole in the seabed. New Atlantis is safely sealed off and humankind is safe!

As the Barracuda's damaged shield and cloaking systems come back online, you turn to Shen. "Are you OK?" you ask.

She nods.

"Let's go home..."

Go to 50.

You decide that reinforcements could take too long, and head into the rift to find Shen.

Carefully you pilot the Barracuda past the Atlantean forces guarding the entrance. The cloaking device works much better than stealth mode — that was only able to fool long-range sensors. With the cloaking device, your enemies can't see you at all!

You head into the water below the Earth's seabed. The depths are lit up by the planet's molten core that seeps from huge volcanoes, which bubble and boil the water. You are amazed at the hundreds of strange plants and creatures that inhabit this world.

A patrol of Atlantean cavalry, mounted on cyborg seahorses, passes by. They are unaware of your presence.

You see a shoal of huge shark-like creatures heading towards you. There are hundreds of them!

To steer away from the shoal, go to 49.

If you wish to take the Barracuda through the shoal, go to 5.

"I have left my sub outside the city. It has a cloaking device, so you will not find it. Inside the vessel is a seaquake device."

Triton looks alarmed.

"Release Shen and allow us to leave your city,

or it will detonate and destroy your kingdom."

"But you will also be killed," Triton points out. "I think you are bluffing."

"Are you sure?" you reply. "I have already defeated your commanders and made my way here. I am not someone to be taken lightly."

"But what is to stop you detonating the device and destroying my kingdom once you have left?"

"I give you my word," you say. "I will not destroy your kingdom."

"But you are forgetting one thing," says Triton. "I have a hostage, and I will kill her if you do not reveal the location of your vessel." He holds his sword against Shen's throat.

If you wish to give Triton the location of the Barracuda, go to 2.

If you don't want to, go to 21.

31

You pick up a homing device, so that you can locate the Barracuda on your return, and head out of the airlock on the DPV. Ahead of you is a line of submarines queuing to get in

through the gates to New Atlantis. The next ship in line is a Lionfish destroyer.

As you are deciding what to do, you see an Atlantean Ray fighter patrol speeding in your direction.

If you think you should hide from the Ray fighters, go to 44.

If you want to stop and see where the Ray fighters are heading, go to 15.

32

As the cyborg shark moves in for the kill you open fire with your jet gun. Steel darts flash through the water and strike home. But the shark continues its attack! The darts are useless against such a creature.

You spin the DPV around in an attempt to escape, but the machine is far too slow. You scream out in agony as the shark's deadly teeth crunch down on your legs. Mercifully the pain doesn't last long as you drift off into the darkness...

Your plan to get into New Atlantis didn't work. Go back to 1.

You turn the Barracuda towards the Atlantean patrol and fire a salvo of torpedoes.

They detonate, but only take out a couple of Atlanteans. The others head towards you at speed. Although they can't see the Barracuda, they can see its shape outlined by the shoal! Within seconds the patrol of Atlanteans has surrounded the super sub and leapt onto the hull. You can hear metal clanging noises as they attempt to break in.

You hit jet boost and leave the patrol far behind. However, your relief is only temporary.

"Mines attached to the hull!" warns the Barracuda's voice.

Your captured defensive shield is designed to stop a torpedo attack, but the Atlanteans have set magnetic mines to explode inside it! Before you can do anything there is a series of deafening explosions. The Barracuda is split open and water pours in sending you to oblivion.

Your quest is over. Go back to 1.

"We need to get to the hole in the seabed," you say. You cancel the seaquake device's countdown and hit jet boost. The Barracuda shoots away.

Although Triton can't see the super sub, he somehow manages to follow you.

"How does he know where we are?" you demand.

"That cyborg Tiger shark can sense tiny changes in pressure," Shen says. "It's following the wake from the Barracuda's propulsion system."

As you speed through the water towards the hole in the seabed, the Barracuda gives a warning. "Enemy ahead."

You cut speed and switch on the scanner and gasp. There are hundreds of Atlantean ships blocking the way between you and the exit!

If you wish to attack them, go to 25.
To try to sneak past the enemy, go to 41.

35

You decide to take the DPV as it is less visible than the sub-aqua bike.

You guide the Barracuda nearer to the dome, carefully avoiding any Atlantean ships. You set the super sub onto the ocean floor and turn off the engines.

You arm yourself with your jet gun and self-propelled grenades. As you change into your aquasuit and prepare the Mer DPV, you think about the seaquake device that Admiral Merrow gave to you. You have to decide whether to take it with you or leave it in the Barracuda and set it to detonate in case you don't get back alive.

If you wish to take the seaquake device, go to 10.

If you want to leave it in the Barracuda, go to 27.

36

The Atlanteans move in as you fire two grenades with your jet gun. They explode, taking out several enemies. The others return fire with their dart guns.

You just manage to avoid the stream of deadly steel barbs and again fire more grenades.

You are outnumbered, but fighting well — until more Atlanteans arrive and open fire. You try to avoid the stream of steel, but it is hopeless. The metal tears into your aquasuit and your lifeless body floats away.

You nearly made it into New Atlantis! To try again, go back to 1.

37

You follow the Starfish cruiser from a distance.

After some hours of travelling, the Barracuda displays the 3-D image of a vast underwater ridge rising from the seabed. In the centre of the ridge is a huge canyon. It glows yellow and red, lighting up the dark sea, but is hidden by thick seaweed.

The Atlantean ship heads down into the rift. Sentry turrets and a squadron of Ray fighters guard the approach. This is the hole in the seabed that you've been searching for!

If you wish to head into the canyon,
go to 29.

If you wish to report the location of
the rift to ORCA, go to 20.

38

You are bundled into the Flying fish hovercraft
and are soon on your way to Triton's HQ. You
keep a nervous eye on the Atlantean soldiers,
in case they attack.

Eventually, you arrive at an enormous
palace and are hurried into a vast room.
Rows and rows of armed guards almost fill
the whole space. You are pushed through the
crowd until you reach the far end of the room.
Standing there waiting for you is Triton. He
has a huge grin on his face. Next to the King of
the Atlanteans is Shen. She is bound by thick
chains. You move forward and smile, trying to
reassure her.

Triton speaks mockingly, "So, puny human.
Here you are, alone and weaponless. You claim
that you can destroy my city. How are you
going to do that, exactly?"

If you brought the seaquake device with you, go to 46.

If you left the seaquake device in the Barracuda, go to 30.

39

You decide to take the sub-aqua bike.

You guide the Barracuda nearer to the dome, carefully avoiding any Atlantean ships. You set the super sub onto the ocean floor and turn off the engines.

You prepare the sub-aqua bike and arm it with sea dart missiles. You change into your aquasuit and think about the seaquake device that Admiral Merrow gave to you. You have to decide whether to take it with you, or leave it in the Barracuda and set it to detonate in case you don't get back alive.

To take the seaquake device, go to 10.

To leave it in the Barracuda, go to 27.

40

Ignoring the shark, and carefully avoiding the other Atlantean guards patrolling the entrance

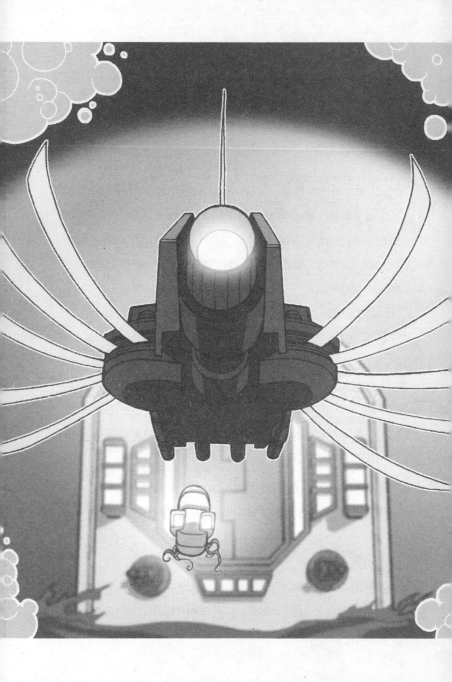

to the dome, you move towards the Lionfish destroyer. You pass by the enemy subs and finally reach the destroyer. You inspect it carefully, trying to identify the best place to hide.

If you wish to hide at the rear of the Lionfish destroyer, go to 48.

If you wish to hide beneath the destroyer, go to 26.

If you wish to hide at the side of the destroyer, go to 19.

41

You move forward slowly. Suddenly the whole sea is lit up.

"Electric eel mines deployed," warns the Barracuda. The sea is filled with sparks of electricity. The Barracuda is caught up in the electric storm. Circuits fizz and crackle. Smoke pours from the control systems.

"The cloaking device is compromised and the defensive shield is down," says Shen. "We are visible to the enemy!"

"Enemy weapon systems locking on," Shen warns. "The Royal cyborg Tiger shark is four

hundred metres away and closing. Triton is moving in for the kill!"

"How far to the exit?" you ask.

"Three hundred metres," replies Shen.

To turn to attack Triton, go to 9.

If you want to jet boost for the exit, go to 28.

42

You decide to wait for reinforcements.

An hour later the comms system bursts into life. Admiral Merrow appears. He looks sad. "I have just received a message from Triton," he says. "He is threatening to kill Shen if he is attacked. My daughter means the world to me. He knows that we took the cloaking device from Captain Tempest. I am sorry that I have to do this."

"Do what?" you ask.

"I have remotely deactivated the Barracuda's cloaking device. I am sorry..." The link breaks off.

Alarms suddenly sound inside the cockpit. "Incoming attack."

Without the cloaking device, the Barracuda
is easily spotted by the surrounding subs.
Dozens of torpedoes hit the super sub as you
turn to escape.

"Defensive shield damaged," reports the
Barracuda.

You are about to launch countermeasures
when the cockpit implodes, taking you to a
watery grave.

You've been betrayed! Go back to 1.

43

You realise that there is no chance of escape,
so you drop your weapons and hold up your
hands in surrender. An Atlantean moves in and
jabs you with an electro lance. You feel a surge
of pain, then pass out.

Go to 23.

44

You spin around to find a place to hide, but the
Ray fighters spot you moving and open fire. Two
deadly torpedoes shoot towards you.

There is a flash of light and then a brief roar
as the torpedoes explode, sending you to a
watery death.

Your quest has failed! Start again at 1.

45

"Abandon the attack," you say.

At that moment the computer's alarm begins
to wail. "Incoming SMART torpedoes," it warns.

You realise that although the Atlanteans
can't see you, they have followed the track of
your torpedoes and worked out your position.

You spin the Barracuda, and the incoming
torpedoes speed by and detonate harmlessly.
Although the cloaking device has saved you,
the enemy knows you are here! What are you
going to do?

If you wish to continue the fight, go to 25.
To try to trick the enemy, go to 8.

46

You unclip the seaquake device from your
aquasuit. Shen's eyes widen in horror — she
knows what this is!

"It's a seaquake device," you tell Triton.

Triton's eyes narrow. "And what are you going to do with it?" you ask.

"Nothing, if you release Shen and allow us to leave your city," you reply.

"And if I refuse?"

"Then I will destroy your kingdom."

Triton begins to laugh. "You dare to threaten me!" Without warning he thrusts his trident into you. Shen lets out a scream and pulls away from her captors as you drop to the floor.

You know you are dying, but you still have the seaquake device.

"Goodbye, Shen," you whisper. She holds onto your hand tightly.

Before Triton can move, there is a blinding flash of light, and then nothing.

You've destroyed New Atlantis and saved Earth, but paid a high price. Try to stay alive — go back to 1 to begin your quest again.

47

You speed up and move ahead of the shoal. The Atlantean patrol approaches, but because

the shape of the Barracuda has disappeared
and you are still cloaked, they cannot see
where you are. You breathe a sigh of relief,
but you are not out of danger yet.

Go to 49.

48

You move towards the rear of the Lionfish
destroyer and settle in behind it. The gates
to the dome open up and the vessel's engines
burst into life, churning up the water.

You are caught in the whirlpool created by
the engines. You spin around and around, out
of control.

Desperately, you throttle up the DPV to
try to break free of the raging torrent. It is
useless. Your body is pierced as you are thrust
onto the destroyer's spiked fins.

You've been skewered! Go back to 1.

49

You steer to the left and soon leave the
Atlantean patrol behind.

The whole area is a hive of activity. Turtle

troopships and Crab tanks scuttle along the ocean floor and Ray fighters speed past you, all unaware of your presence. You decide to follow them.

Sometime later you see a vast transparent dome sitting on the ocean floor. Within the dome is a great city with many strange-looking buildings.

"New Atlantis," you whisper.

You have found the realm of Triton! Now you have to work out how to get into the city.

If you wish to follow the line of Atlantean ships, go to 22.

If you wish to scan the entrance to New Atlantis, go to 13.

50

Some time later you arrive back in Mer City.
Shen's father and Admiral Crabbe are there
to greet you. "New Atlantis is once again
sealed off," says Merrow. "We will monitor the
Atlanteans more carefully, and make sure that
they do not break out again. But now Triton
and his commanders have gone, there will be
no one to stir up trouble."

"Great work," says Admiral Crabbe. "We
couldn't have defeated Triton without you
and Shen."

"Don't forget the Barracuda," you smile.
"That is one amazing piece of machinery!"

Crabbe nods in approval. "We want you to
continue to work with ORCA. Are you up for it?"

"Will Shen be co-pilot?" you ask.

"Of course!"

"Then I accept!"

There will be more challenges, but with your
skill and the Barracuda you feel ready for any
new threats that might emerge from the sea.
The Earth is once again safe!

You are a hero!

TOP SECRET: Barracuda – sub-aqua bike

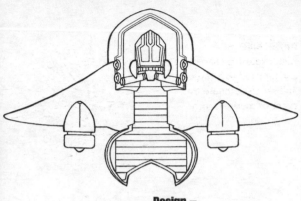

Design –

Intended for short-range travel. Hard for enemies to detect it on scanners because of its streamlined shape.

Armament –

Sea dart missiles.

TOP SECRET: ORCA weapons technology

Urchin mine –
High-explosive charge that can be fixed to a target and set to detonate by timer or motion sensor.

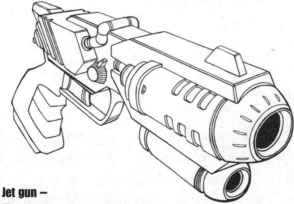

Jet gun –
Short-range weapon that is capable of firing barbed projectiles underwater. Also has a launcher that can fire flares, and self-propelled stun and high explosive grenades.

About the 2Steves

"The 2Steves" are
Britain's most popular
writing double act
for young people,
specialising in comedy
and adventure. They

perform regularly in schools and libraries,
and at festivals, taking the power of words
and story to audiences of all ages.

Together they have written many books,
including the *Crime Team* and *iHorror* series.

About the illustrator: Jack Lawrence

Jack Lawrence is a successful freelance
comics illustrator, working on titles such as
A.T.O.M., Cartoon Network, *Doctor Who
Adventures*, *2000 AD*, *Gogos Mega Metropolis*
and *Spider-Man Tower of Power*. He also works
as a freelance toy designer.

Jack lives in Maidstone in Kent with
his partner and two cats.

Have you completed the other I HERO Quests?

Battle with aliens in Tyranno Quest:

AIR BLAST
Steve Barlow · Steve Skidmore
978 1 4451 0875 9 pb
978 1 4451 1345 6 ebook

FIRE STORM
Steve Barlow · Steve Skidmore
978 1 4451 0876 6 pb
978 1 4451 1346 3 ebook

ICE STRIKE
Steve Barlow · Steve Skidmore
978 1 4451 0877 3 pb
978 1 4451 1347 0 ebook

EARTH ATTACK
Steve Barlow · Steve Skidmore
978 1 4451 0878 0 pb
978 1 4451 1348 7 ebook

Defeat the Red Queen in Blood Crown Quest:

SANDS OF BLOOD
Steve Barlow · Steve Skidmore
978 1 4451 1499 6 pb
978 1 4451 1503 0 ebook

DRAGON MOUNTAIN
Steve Barlow · Steve Skidmore
978 1 4451 1500 9 pb
978 1 4451 1504 7 ebook

DEMON SEA
Steve Barlow · Steve Skidmore
978 1 4451 1501 6 pb
978 1 4451 1505 4 ebook

CITY OF THE DEAD
Steve Barlow · Steve Skidmore
978 1 4451 1502 3 pb
978 1 4451 1506 1 ebook

Also by the 2Steves...

978 0 7496 9283 4 pb
978 1 4451 0843 8 eBook

A millionaire is found at his luxury
island home – dead! But no one can
work out how he died. You must get
to Skull Island and solve the mystery
before his killer escapes.

978 0 7496 9284 1 pb
978 1 4451 0844 5 eBook

The daughter of a Hong Kong
businessman has been kidnapped.
You must find her, but who took
her and why? You must crack the
case, before it's too late!

978 0 7496 9286 5 pb
978 1 4451 0845 2 eBook

You must solve the clues to stop
a terrorist attack in London.
But who is planning the attack,
and when will it take place? It's
a race against time!

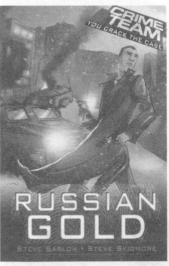

978 0 7496 9285 8 pb
978 1 4451 0846 9 eBook

An armoured convoy has been
attacked in Moscow and hundreds
of gold bars stolen. But who was
behind the raid, and where is the
gold? Get the clues - get the gold.